Stomach contents everywhere . . .

"Cockroaches!" I yelled. I spit my mouthful of food out on the table. The slimy, half-chewed wad that landed there was definitely moving. I could see one cockroach that'd been cut in half.

I knew where the other half of that cockroach was.

"*Aaargh!* There are roaches in the food!" Zoner shouted.

Allie was the first to blow. Her eyes changed from blue to green behind her glasses. Her throat started doing the gack dance. Then she emitted. She extruded.

"*G-g-g-ovf-bleah!*" It was stomach contents everywhere, all over the table and dripping off the sides.

At which point my stomach began to squish and squirm. I tried to hold back, but it was too late. I was in the final countdown.

THE GREAT PUKE-OFF

BY
PAT POLLARI

BANTAM BOOKS
NEW YORK • TORONTO • LONDON • SYDNEY • AUCKLAND

To Michael

RL 4, age 008-012

THE GREAT PUKE-OFF
A Bantam Book / July 1996

*Barf-O-Rama™ and the Barf-O-Rama Logo™ are
trademarks of Daniel Weiss Associates, Inc.*

*Produced by Daniel Weiss Associates, Inc.
33 West 17th Street
New York, NY 10011*

ISBN: 0-553-48406-0

Published simultaneously in the United States and Canada

Bantam Books are published by Bantam Books, a division of Bantam
Doubleday Dell Publishing Group, Inc. Its trademark, consisting of the
words "Bantam Books" and the portrayal of a rooster, is Registered in U.S.
Patent and Trademark Office and in other countries. Marca Registrada.
Bantam Books, 1540 Broadway, New York, New York 10036.

PRINTED IN THE UNITED STATES OF AMERICA

OPM   0 9 8 7 6 5 4 3 2 1

ONE

Nothing ever made Lester Peebles sick. We always said he had a heave-proof stomach. Things that would make any normal person spew gumbo meant nothing to Lester. I mean, I've seen Lester outside on a really cold day actually licking his own snotsicles like they were ice cream. Nothing could make that boy launch his lunch.

But that was before the gross-out war started.

Let me make one thing clear right up front: we did not start the gross-out war with those evil twins, Darren and Debbie. Darren and Debbie started it all. Darren and Debbie fired the first shot.

I'll admit our group (that would be Allie

1

Hogan, Zoner Russo, Lester, and me, Mark Fine) had never gotten along very well with Darren and Debbie and their friends, Willie Leroux and Sara "Skank" McPhee. And when I say that we had never gotten along very well, what I mean is we mostly hated each other.

Two important facts I have to tell you. First, "Skank" is not some cruel nickname we made up for Sara. She made it up. She wants people to call her Skank. Which kind of tells you what's going on with her.

The other important thing you need to know is the last name of Darren and Debbie, which is Chapman. Why is that important? Because our school principal is also named Chapman. Yes, Darren and Debbie are the principal's kids. Which means every teacher at the school thinks they are just the most perfect little angels.

I happen to know the twins are as rotten as a tuna salad sandwich that slips down between the cushions of your couch and stays there for a month. But no one believes me, of course, because supposedly I'm a troublemaker.

Me, a troublemaker? Sweet, kind, decent Mark Fine? Just because it was me who glued the door of the teachers' lounge shut so they had to be rescued by the fire department? I wouldn't call that making trouble, exactly. More like a practical joke.

But ever since then, every teacher at school thinks I'm the troublemaker and Darren and Debbie are perfect. What they don't know is that it was the twins who flushed twenty pounds of kidney beans down the toilets. The beans collected in the pipes, swelled up from the water, and eventually broke the pipes. Which caused sewage to spill all over the lower floors and even pelted the science teacher, Mr. Bush, with a great load of brown substance.

I'll admit, it was funny seeing Mr. Bush standing there dripping yellow stain with a chocolate log on his head. But I did not do it. I laughed my hinder off, but I did not do it.

Just the same, I got punished. By Mr. Chapman. The father of the evil twins. Everyone just assumed it was poor innocent Mark.

There is no justice in fifth grade.

So anyway, my friends and I were not exactly buddies with the twins and their friends. But it didn't come to total, all-out war until the Day of the Great Burrito Barf.

We're in the cafeteria, Zoner and Allie and Lester and me.

I'm going through the line—you know, getting the usual cafeteria slop loaded on my tray. When who do I see standing behind the counter, wearing one of those plastic Baggies on his head? Willie Leroux.

I'll explain Willie this way: if Darren and Debbie were the Addams Family, Willie would be Lurch. He's the closest thing I've ever seen to an actual Klingon.

So here's Willie Leroux, who looks like he's a tenth grader, and probably should be, standing behind the line, dishing out burritos.

"Willie, what are you doing back there?" I asked.

He shrugged. "I'm the new student lunchroom volunteer."

I think, okay. There's always some student working with the lunch ladies to earn extra brownie points. But since when would a creature like Willie Leroux be a volunteer for anything? So I'm suspicious.

But not suspicious enough.

The food is the usual stuff we always have on Mexican day: two burritos and some rice and some of those slimy refried beans. And we're all sitting at the table, munching away, when all of a sudden Allie screams.

"There are . . . there are . . ." She couldn't even say the words. All she could do was point. She was pointing at the burritos we'd all been eating. They looked like pretty normal burritos to me, except that when you looked real close you could see that under the tortillas something was MOVING.

And when you cut into one, things were coming out. CRAWLING out.

If only I had looked before I took that first big—strangely crunchy—bite.

"Cockroaches!" I yelled. I spit my mouthful of food out on the table. The slimy, half-chewed wad landed there in the middle of the table. The mouthful of half-chewed food was definitely moving. I could see one cockroach that'd been cut in half.

I knew where the other half of that cockroach was.

"*Aaargh!* There are roaches in the food!" Zoner shouted.

Allie was the first to blow. Her eyes changed from blue to green behind her glasses. Her throat started doing the gack dance. Then she emitted. She extruded.

"*G-g-g-ovf-bleah!*" It was stomach contents everywhere, all over the table and dripping off the sides.

At which point my stomach began to squish and squirm. I tried to hold back, but it was too late. Between the fact that I had eaten cockroaches and the fact that Allie's steaming puke was all over the table, I was in the final countdown.

I looked across the table at Zoner. His eyes were popping out of his head and his face was red from trying to hold it down. But we both knew there was no way. We had to blow.

Zoner and I launched at the same time.

"*G-g-g-ovf-bleah!*" The spew streams met in midair and rained down on the table.

Naturally people were looking at us. Wouldn't you? So I explained. "There are roaches in the burritos!"

I imagine I looked pretty wild. There was gack dripping from my mouth. Allie, who is normally kind of pretty and has nice red hair, now had chunks of spew in the ends of her hair. Zoner looked like someone who was about to die. He usually looks that way, but this time it was worse.

The whole cafeteria was staring at us. They didn't want to believe what I was saying. But by then the stench of steaming puke was wafting through the room.

"Bugs!" I yelled. "Bug burritos!"

First this guy at the next table blew. Then a girl two tables over. Then two kids at once. The momentum was building, faster, faster!

The whole cafeteria went nuts, heaving and gacking and extruding large quantities of stomach contents.

The sound of all those people making the awful vocals of vomit was something I would never forget. Everyone woofed.

All except Lester Peebles.

Lester Peebles just picked through his burrito. He used his fork to pick out the two roaches squirming there and squished them to death with his spoon. Then he calmly ate his food.

We all just stared at him.

"How can you eat that?" Allie cried as she wiped her dripping mouth on her sleeve.

Lester smiled. You could see the food in his mouth when he smiled. You could see that there were tiny kicking legs and tiny wiggling antennas in the food in his mouth.

"I like burritos," Lester said.

That's Lester for you. Nothing. Nothing can make him spew.

Well . . . almost nothing.

TWO

It took exactly thirteen minutes after all the heaving and spewing was done for Mr. Chapman to have me hauled down to his office.

I said, "Hi, Mr. Chapman."

He said, "Mark FINE, you SIT in that CHAIR and SHUT your mouth UNTIL I ask you to speak. And THEN you tell me the TRUTH, or so help me, I'll . . . I'll . . ."

He never did say exactly what he would do. Maybe because he was grinding his teeth too hard to actually speak for a while. I was kind of worried about him, the way his face was all red and his eyes were practically popping out of his head. I mean, I had seen enough grossness for one day. I sure didn't need Mr.

Chapman's eyeballs suddenly exploding or something.

He reached for a phone book and I thought maybe he was going to look up a number. But instead he just grabbed it and slowly ripped it in half. I never knew Mr. Chapman was that strong.

I think he was upset.

He glared at me with his big popping eyes. "You've done it this time, Mark. You've stepped way over the line. WAAAY over the line."

"Mr. Chapman, I had nothing to do with putting cockroaches in the burritos," I cried. "Really!"

He pointed his finger at me. It was shaking. And so was I. "You were the one who started it. The teachers who were monitoring the lunchroom all say the same thing—Mark Fine yelled that there were cockroaches in the food."

"I did, but . . . but I mean, there WERE cockroaches in the food. It was bug burritos, Mr. Chapman. Even for school food that's bad."

"Oh, really? Then how is it that the only cockroaches anyone found were at YOUR table? It seems only YOU and YOUR friends had infested burritos."

"Excuse me?" I said.

"That's right. We CHECKED. No one else had bugs in their burritos. Just you and your little friends, Mark. And do you know what that makes me think?"

"That . . . that there's been a terrible mistake?"

"Oh, there's been a mistake, all right," he said in this scary little whispering voice. "Oh, yessss, there's been a mistake. Your mistake. I know what happened. You planted a few bugs in your own food so that you could start a panic! And you succeeded. Do you know that so far the janitors have filled seventeen buckets with vomit? SEVENTEEN BUCKETS OF BARF, Mark Fine. And all your doing!"

"But . . . but . . . but . . . ," I said.

"But nothing," he growled. "I can't prove it yet, Mark. But I will. You can count on it. I WILL find the proof that you are behind this . . . this OUTRAGE. And when I do . . ." He cackled. He actually cackled and rubbed his hands together. I would say he looked totally insane, only he was way past totally insane.

11

"Now get OUT," he said. "Your days are numbered. My eyes are ON you. I'll find the proof, and I will DESTROY you!"

I ran for it. That seemed like the smartest thing to do, just get out of that office. I mean, I'd been to Mr. Chapman's office before when he was mad at me. But those other times he had never actually said he would destroy me. I had to take that seriously.

Outside the office my friends were waiting for me. Zoner was looking as angry as he ever looks, which isn't very angry. And Allie was looking angry in a cute sort of way. Lester still had no idea what we were all so upset about.

"Did Chapman ream you?" Zoner asked.

"Basically he threatened to kill me and use ME to make burritos," I said, exaggerating only slightly.

"This is so unfair," Allie said. "We figured out what happened. It was Willie Leroux. He was working behind the lunch counter."

I was about to say something sarcastic, along the lines of "No duh, Nancy Drew," but I like Allie. So I just said, "Yeah, I know. Mr. Chapman says we were the only ones with bug burritos. It was Willie, all right. And where there's a Willie—"

12

"There's a Darren and Debbie," Allie completed my sentence.

"Did I hear someone mention us?" a voice said.

We all spun around. There they were: the evil twins, in the flesh. Darren has this incredibly light, wispy blond hair and eyes that are so light blue it's almost like he doesn't have any pupils. Debbie is exactly the same, except her hair is longer. They sort of remind me of those two twin girls who used to be on that TV show. But not quite that awful.

"We know you set this whole thing up," I said, pointing my finger at them.

Darren and Debbie just laughed. They have these weird, high-pitched laughs that remind you of fingernails scratching down a blackboard.

"Us?" Debbie said, pretending to be shocked. "WE did it? How could you possibly suspect US? Everyone knows YOU are the troublemaker, Mark Fine."

"Yeah," Darren agreed. "We have straight-A averages and every teacher loves us and our father's the principal. How could we possibly do anything as gross as stuffing cockroaches in your food?"

And then they both laughed their creepy laughs.

They did it, all right. And they knew we knew they did it. And they didn't care, because they thought they were totally safe.

"This isn't over," I said, trying to sound threatening. "Payback will be painful."

"Yeah, we're going to get you back twice as good as you got us," Allie said, backing me up.

"Oooooh," Darren said. "I guess I'll just live in fear. Won't you live in fear, Debbie?"

"Terror. Total terror." Debbie grinned.

"Come on, guys," I said. "Let the identical creeps think they've won. We'll deal with them later."

We marched off down the hall, swaggering and trying to look cool. But the annoying laughter of the evil twins followed us down the hallway.

"So what are we going to do?" Zoner asked me.

"We're going to get them back, that's what we're going to do," I said.

"So . . . like how?"

I thought about it for a moment. "They grossed us out, right?"

"Not me," Lester said.

Allie rolled her eyes. "They sure grossed me out."

"Okay, then." I stopped when we were around the corner, where the twins couldn't see us anymore. My friends gathered around. "They used grossness, right? So we'll use grossness. We'll show them just how gross gross can be."

"But how can we outgross the twins?" Zoner wondered.

"We'll think about it. We'll work on it and plan, just like they did. We have to organize. We have to study grossness and do our grossness homework. And I don't mean halfway studying like we do for schoolwork. THIS is important."

I stuck my hand out in the middle of the circle. "Are you with me?" I cried.

Allie clasped her hand over mine. "I'm in," she said.

Zoner clasped his hand over hers. "I'm in, too," he said.

We all three looked at Lester.

But Lester was busy. His right index finger was buried in his nose, all the way to the second knuckle. He concentrated as he dug away. Finally he drew out a long, green nose noodle.

He held the slimy wad up to the light to see it better.

"Lester," Allie said, sounding disgusted.

He seemed surprised to see that we were all watching him. He looked around for a place to wipe the mucilage. But he couldn't find anything, so he calmly stuck his finger in his mouth and licked it clean.

Then he prepared to join our handclasp.

"That's okay, Lester," I said quickly. "You're in."

THREE

Our first planning session took place at my house, up in my room. I have a pretty cool room with posters and stuff all over the walls. And I have it all to myself because I just have one little sister, Krista, and she's really little. Little, as in she's still a baby.

"Okay," Zoner said as he flopped back on my bed. "What's the plan?"

"One thing for sure," Allie said. "We have to get all four of them, just like they got all four of us. We can't just get Darren and Debbie. We need to get Skank and Willie, too."

"Skank?" Lester asked. "Why do we have to get her?"

"She's one of them," I said. "You know she was in on it somehow. She probably supplied the roaches."

Lester seemed a little troubled, but that's nothing new. In case you haven't guessed it yet, Lester is slightly unusual.

"Let's just beat them up," Zoner suggested.

Allie and I rolled our eyes. "I don't think so," I said. "First of all, it's too obvious. Second of all, between Willie and Skank they'd kick our hinders."

"No, we need something . . . great," Allie said. Her eyes were all aglow. "We need something incredible. We need something so sickening, so disgusting, so twisted that even if we live a thousand years, people will still say, 'This was their grossest hour!'"

"Wow," Zoner agreed.

I was in awe of her. It was like listening to one of those history guys in the videos. Like George Jefferson or General Custard.

"Allie's right," I said. "We must choose our plan carefully. Starting with . . . the substance."

"Which substance?" Lester asked, suddenly interested. "Mucilage?"

"How about whiff?" Zoner said.

18

"I don't know if whiff is an actual sub-stance," I said. "Whiff is like blatt. I mean, it's a gas. I don't know how we could deliver whiff. That would require all of us to have perfect flatuosity."

"What's the problem?" Lester asked. And then he fired a multipopper that seemed to go on and on. No one can play the under thunder like Lester.

"*Ghah!*" Allie cried as the stench wafted to her.

We opened the window and I made Lester go sit by it.

"Lester, we don't need any more demon-strations, okay?" I said. He just grinned.

"How about barf?" Zoner suggested. "I mean, it would serve them right."

I nodded. "Vomit is always good," I agreed. "Vomit always makes you want to spew. It's like vomit creates vomit, almost. I'll bet it's some scientific principle." I felt I might be close to an important idea there, but I knew I had to stick to business. Later on there might be time for such scientific questions, but not now.

Just then from down the hall we heard a loud wailing sound. Krista.

"Is that your little sister?" Allie asked.

"Yeah. But don't worry," I said. "It just means she needs her diaper changed."

The four of us froze. That was it. We looked at each other, our eyes bright.

"Ordure," Allie said.

"Pooptonium," Zoner agreed.

"Yes, that's it," I cried. "Diaper gravy!"

"There's only one problem," Allie said. "Darren and Debbie aren't dumb. They know we're coming after them. They'll be prepared."

"You're right," Zoner said, looking dismayed.

"A distraction," I said. "We hit them with something simple. Something they'll see right through. That way they'll be all cocky and confident when we really hit them."

"Besides," Lester said. "It will take at least a day to collect enough diaper gravy. We'll need a pretty large amount."

Count on Lester to know that.

The next day right before lunch Mrs. Grady, our regular teacher, made a big announcement.

"Class, I have something very special to tell you."

I groaned, because I figured she was announcing a test.

"Stop groaning, Mark," Mrs. Grady said, giving me the evil eye. "I think even you will enjoy this announcement. Due to the unfortunate incident in the cafeteria yesterday, Mr. Chapman has decided that all the students who were there should be given a very special treat."

"Not more burritos, I hope," I said under my breath.

"We are going to take a field trip!" I was expecting her to say a field trip to the museum or something. But she said, "A field trip to Adventure Land!"

"Adventure Land! No way!" I cried. Adventure Land was only the coolest amusement park, filled with the most extreme rides. They had three different roller coasters and two water slides and a whole raft of other stuff.

This was most excellent. I caught Zoner's eye across the room. He gave me a thumbs-up sign.

I couldn't believe I would ever be grateful for anything Mr. Chapman did, but this was definitely cool.

The bell rang for lunch, but the cafeteria was closed. We all knew about it, though, so we'd brought bag lunches. They'd announced it on the radio yesterday. Seems there were inspectors from the state who had to come in and figure out why there were roaches in the burritos. I could have told them, but they didn't ask. Plus, with about two inches of barf on the floor, I guess it took a while to clean up. I mean, it was like a barf wading pool in the cafeteria.

The bag lunches gave us the opportunity for our "diversion." We called the diversion Plan A. Plan B would be the real attack.

It was a nice day outside, so they told us to have lunch in the grassy area behind the gym. They have some picnic tables there, but there weren't enough for all the kids, so most of us just sat on the grass.

Darren, Debbie, Willie, and Skank were sitting in a circle under one of the trees. I looked at Allie, Zoner, and Lester and nodded. Plan A was ready to go into effect.

The four of us, clutching our lunch bags, headed straight for the evil twins and their little group. We had rehearsed the whole plan, so we knew it would work.

Debbie spotted us as we got close. But before she could say anything, Zoner pretended to trip. He stumbled toward the twins, and Allie and I raced to grab him before he could fall.

Zoner fell on the grass, right between Debbie and Skank. I tripped over Darren and practically ended up on Willie's lap. Which is a fairly disgusting thing all by itself.

It was total chaos. The twins jumped up and started yelling at us. "You dorks! You clumsy morons!"

Skank glared and said, "Hey, get offa me, you loser."

"Sorry," I yelled. "So sorry!" But as I tried to stand up, naturally I slipped again and knocked Willie over on his back. Zoner said, "Whoa, dudes, sorry. Man, am I ever clumsy." Then he tripped right into Darren and knocked him on his buttal region.

Meanwhile Lester and Allie hung back from the confusion. They worked fast, first opening Darren's blue nylon lunch bag, then Debbie's pink nylon lunch bag, then Willie's plastic grocery-store bag, and finally Skank's grease-stained paper bag.

It was so smooth it was ninja. It was like some perfectly timed spy thing. In fact, I was a little worried it might be too smooth. Like maybe the twins wouldn't catch on.

"Get away, you creeps," Debbie screamed at Zoner and me.

Finally Zoner and I got ourselves untangled and stood back. We brushed ourselves off. "Hey, you guys don't have to get so mean just because we tripped accidentally," I said.

"Yeah," Zoner agreed.

The four of us marched off like we were very offended. But we stopped maybe twenty feet away, where we could still see the twins and they could still see us.

I saw Darren looking at us with those creepy, almost-all-white eyes of his. He nudged Debbie and she stared at us, too. Willie opened his bag and reached inside.

"No!" Debbie suddenly yelled. She reached over, snatched Willie's bag from him, and threw it away. Then she picked up her own lunch bag, stood up, and opened it slowly. She raised it high and turned it over. Out fell a sandwich—I think it was baloney and cheese—and an apple and a Twinkie.

Oh, and the worms fell out, too. A great, glistening, squirming, slithering mass of bloodworms, all fat and bloated.

FOUR

"**P**ick those up," Debbie ordered Skank. Skank obeyed. Like Lester, Skank has no fear of grossness. She just picked up the closest wad of worms and held it, writhing, in her bare hand.

"Come with me," Debbie said. Darren followed her, along with Willie, Skank, and the worms.

I stood my ground as they approached. Lester was staring at the worms—or maybe at Skank, I couldn't be sure. Allie and Zoner stood with me.

"I believe these are yours," Darren said, pointing at the worms.

"Not originally," I said. "We got them from your underwear drawer."

"Very funny," Darren said. But I could see

he was mad because he couldn't think of a funny comeback.

"You guys are pathetic," Debbie sneered. "This is the best you can do? Worms in our bag lunches? It's not even slightly original. And we didn't fall for it."

"That whole distraction with you guys tripping all over us was so lame," Darren said, agreeing with his sister. "Like we wouldn't figure out you were up to something?"

"Face it," Debbie said. "You guys are losers."

Debbie and Darren looked at each other and laughed their identical laughs. Then they took off across the field, still laughing. Willie went after them. Only Skank remained behind. She seemed to be fascinated by the worms she was holding.

"Cool, aren't they?" Lester asked her.

She nodded. "You want 'em back?" She held out her hand.

Lester blushed. "No, you can keep them."

"Thanks," Skank said, and started off after the twins and Willie. A few seconds later we heard Debbie's high-pitched shriek, yelling at Skank to throw the stupid worms away.

"That worked perfectly," I said, once the twins were too far away to hear.

26

"Perfectly," Allie agreed.

"Now they think we're total idiots. They won't even be expecting it when we hit them with Plan B."

"Where is Lester?" Allie asked.

It was later that same day, and we were all supposed to hook up at my house to begin Plan B. Zoner was there and Allie, too. We were looking at the black plastic trash cans in my driveway behind the garage.

"I guess we could go ahead and get started," Zoner said. He didn't sound enthusiastic. And I couldn't blame him.

Allie lifted the lid of the nearest trash can. A wave of stench rolled out. It was the special smell of rotting garbage, with the added element of baby diapers.

"Argh," I said. I turned away and tried to find some clean air to breathe.

Allie made gagging noises, too, as she backed away.

"I don't think I should even have to do this part," Zoner complained. "After all, I'm the one who's doing the stuff with my computer. That should be my part."

"No way," I said. "We all have to help with

27

every part of the plan. I came up with the plan, Zoner. You have to do the computer stuff. Besides, Allie's the one who should be complaining. She had to handle the worms this morning for Plan A."

"Okay, okay," Zoner grumbled.

"Maybe there's some other . . . substance . . . we could use," Allie suggested.

I shook my head grimly. "No. This is the substance. The fact that the stench makes you want to woof is what makes it so right."

Sometimes it's not easy being a leader. But I had to stand firm. You need character to lead a group.

"Hey, guys, wait up!" It was Lester, crossing from the far side of the street. "Wait for me."

He came rushing up. "You guys didn't do it without me, did you?"

He was actually worried we'd done all the dirty work without him.

"No, Lester," I said. I patted him on the shoulder. "We waited for you."

"Cool," he said.

"Well, I guess we'd better get started," Allie suggested.

Lester stepped in front of her and quickly lifted the first plastic trash bag up and out of the can. He eagerly unfastened the little twist tie.

We'd only thought there was a stench before. Now, with the bag open, we realized just how much reek we were dealing with.

Allie reeled back. "Ugh, that's odious."

"It's noxious," Zoner agreed.

"That is beyond noxious," I said, covering my mouth with my hand. "It's morbific."

Lester must have misunderstood. Because he grinned and said, "Oh, yes. It certainly is."

"I don't know if I can take this," Allie gasped. "I'm having the urge to purge."

"You have to fight it," I said.

"I don't know if I can help it," Zoner moaned. "I'm going to extrude!"

"Nobody spews," I snapped. I had to put my foot down or we'd never accomplish our plan. "Look. We have a plan, right?"

Allie and Zoner nodded reluctantly. They both looked a little green. They looked like I felt. But I had to be strong.

"Nobody heaves," I said. "There will be no unauthorized guttal explosions. We have a job to do. Do you want Darren and Debbie laughing at us forever because we couldn't do what we set out to do? Do you want to live the rest

29

of your lives knowing that the evil twins kicked your butts?"

Allie and Zoner shook their heads.

"All right, then," I said. "We have to be strong. I'm not going to fail. When I'm an old man like my dad, I want to be able to look back and say, 'Yes, I did it!'"

This inspired Allie and Zoner enough that they gagged down their gullets, gritted their teeth, and prepared to go forward.

Lester looked at me questioningly. I nodded. "Do it, Lester. Dive for diaper."

Lester dug his hand into the garbage. He didn't even look because he didn't have to. He has a special instinct for these things. I saw a look of concentration on his face. Then he nodded and grinned.

"Got one," he announced.

Slowly he drew his hand back out of the garbage bag. In his clenched fist was a Pampers diaper. Or maybe it was a Huggies diaper. I can never tell the difference.

He dived again, and a second diaper came up. And another. Soon Lester had gone through all the garbage and piled seven loaded diapers on the upturned lid of the trash can.

We stood, staring at the white pile.

"Now what, O fearless leader?" Zoner asked me.

"We have to act quickly," I said. "My folks will be home soon. Begin collection." I looked at Lester. "What do you advise for a situation like this?"

He thought for a moment. "We'll need a bucket of warm water—not too much—and a spoon."

I went inside to get the stuff he needed. It was great, breathing normal house odor for a few minutes. I came back out with the bucket and the spoon and right away that stench hit me so hard I almost broke my own rule and had an unauthorized guttal explosion. But I clenched my jaw and fought down the spew.

"Here you go, Lester," I said. I put the bucket on the ground and handed him the spoon.

"Okay," Lester said. "Then let's have diaper number one."

I could have tried to make Allie or Zoner do it, but I knew I couldn't weasel out of all the hard work.

I lifted the first diaper from the pile, using only two fingers of each hand.

31

"Hold it over the bucket," Lester instructed.

I held it over the bucket.

"Now . . . open the diaper," Lester said.

Slowly, slowly, I unfolded the Pamper. I should have looked away, but I couldn't help myself. I stared. I stared hard.

It was yellow and brown and lumpy, like pudding with raisins in it. Diaper gravy. One of the most deadly substances known to man.

I moaned. I saw Allie and Zoner backing away. They had their hands over their mouths.

Lester dug the spoon into the reeking substance. He began scooping it, a spoonful at a time, into the warm water of the bucket.

FIVE

I won't bore you with all the details of how we scraped each diaper into the bucket. Let me just tell you, it was not a fun afternoon.

After we had collected our substance, we took a break over at Zoner's house. Zoner is mostly a goof, except when it comes to computers. The boy is a total genius when it comes to computers.

He used his computer and his modem to get into the school computer. Once inside the school computer, he looked up certain important information. For one thing, we got into the personnel records and found out that our teacher, Mrs. Grady, almost got kicked out her first year of college because she was found with a bunch of other people dancing in a fountain at three in the morning.

That wasn't exactly important information, but I could see where it might be useful someday.

What we were after was something else: locker combinations. Zoner found the file and printed it out, all neat and easy.

"There you go," Zoner announced as the paper came zipping out of his printer.

I scanned down the list. There they were, under the *C*'s: Darren and Debbie Chapman. Then we found Skank and Willie.

"Good job, Zoner," I said. "Now all we need is the balloons."

Everyone groaned, because everyone knew the part that came next was going to be completely vomitous. But we were getting used to stench by now. And we had to have Plan B ready to go.

"Come on, guys," I said. "Victory is within our grasp."

The next morning Allie wasn't on the school bus, and I breathed a sigh of relief. See, if she had been on the bus, that would have meant the plan was in trouble. But somehow she had talked her mom into driving her to school. Allie can talk anyone into anything.

It was important for me to be on the bus, and important for the evil twins to see that I was on the bus. They were sitting close to the front, and I was all the way in back with Zoner and Lester. I checked to see if Old Lady Schwegel, the bus driver, was looking in her mirror. Then I made a quick dash up the aisle and flopped down across from Darren and Debbie.

They looked at me with their creepy eyes and Darren said, "What are you doing up here, loser?"

I gave him a dirty look. I had to give him a dirty look because if I was nice, they'd get suspicious. So I gave them a sneer. Then I leaned over slightly, aimed in their direction, and fired a flatus. "*Blaaat!*"

Normally I don't have the talent of flatuosity. But I was totally inflated that morning, so I could pop it without even straining.

"Creep! Loser!" Darren yelled.

Debbie made a gagging sound and waved the whiff away with her notebook. "You think that was payback?" Debbie laughed. "That was nothing, next to eating cockroaches and then heaving."

"Oh, yeah?" I said. I know, it was a weak comeback. But it was supposed to be weak. I was still making sure that they thought I was a loser.

Also, I wanted to make sure everyone knew I hadn't gotten to school any earlier than the twins. Now everyone on the bus could see that I was right there. They could even smell that I was there.

But it would never occur to them to wonder where *Allie* was. See, Allie was performing our most delicate secret mission.

The bus pulled up in front of school and I made sure Darren and Debbie, as well as Willie and Skank, got off ahead of me and Lester and Zoner.

They walked in through the front door.

We walked in through the front door.

They marched right to their lockers.

We hung back at a safe distance where we could watch. Allie appeared and sidled up next to us. She winked and gave me a thumbs-up.

Good old Allie. I knew she'd come through.

Darren spun the dial on his combination lock. Debbie did the same.

"This is going to be the payback of all time," Zoner said quietly.

I was worried for a minute because it looked like Willie had forgotten his combination. And farther down the hall at her locker, Skank was just plain slow.

The lockers at our school are the tall kind. They each have a shelf at the top that's maybe six inches over your head.

"Get ready," I whispered.

Allie was so excited she grabbed my arm.

Darren's combination clicked. He slammed the lock up. Just a split second behind him, Debbie did the same.

I almost couldn't breathe. I have never been so excited.

Inside Darren's locker was a balloon. There was a string around the mouth of the balloon. The string was attached to the door of the locker. The balloon was inflated almost to the bursting point. But instead of being filled with air, it was filled with liquid.

A brown liquid.

Diaper gravy.

Darren opened his locker door. The door pulled the string. The string yanked the balloon. The balloon slid off the top shelf. It swung down, and out, and straight into Darren Chapman's face.

At almost the same moment an identical balloon hit Debbie.

Both balloons exploded, spewing our own special solution of baby matter and water.

It was a sweet moment.

"Aaaaaargh! Ooooooh! Ghhaaahh!"

The twins screamed in unison. Their faces were a mass of dripping, dribbling, drooling poop. Ordure was in their hair. Ordure was in their ears. Yellow-brown, reeking filth was slithering down their necks and under their clothes.

Willie looked to see what was going on just as his own balloon swung out and smashed into the side of his head. He squealed like a pig. *"Yaagh-gh!"*

But he screamed a little too soon and got a huge mouthful of substance. It was like a second breakfast for Willie: baby matter stew. Pooptonium. Cream of butt product. Chunky style.

I looked down the hall to see Skank. Obviously she'd finally remembered her combination, because she'd been poop ballooned, too. Of course Skank, being Skank, wasn't crying about it like the twins. I guess she's like Lester that way: strong stomach control.

But the twins wouldn't stop screaming. "*Aaah! Uugh! Eeurgh!*" Sure enough, just like Willie, they didn't have the sense to keep their mouths shut.

Let me give you a clue: when there's baby matter dripping all down your face, keep your mouth SHUT.

I watched the chunk that slithered down over Debbie's little nose. I kept watching as it slid down her upper lip. And I watched when it dropped onto her yelling tongue.

I saw Debbie stop screaming. She was frozen. Her mouth snapped shut. Her lips were moving, though. Kind of squirming and wiggling. Her throat was doing the gack dance.

"They're gonna blow!" I cried.

Debbie and Darren both must have heard me because they focused their creepy, evil eyes on me at the same moment. "You!" Darren yelled, pointing at me.

Debbie tried to yell, too, but like I said, her throat was already doing the gack dance.

"*Blllleeeaahhh!*" A stream of cream of barf exploded from her.

And once Debbie had spewed, Darren was right behind her. He was woofing up his organs.

Willie actually heaved into his own locker, which I thought was kind of stupid.

"It was worth it," I told my friends happily. "All the planning and practice. All the hard work. It was so worth it."

I was the happiest person alive.

The only slight cloud on my perfect happiness was that Skank didn't hurl. But I figured three out of four wasn't bad.

SIX

The twins and Willie and Skank were all escorted off to the gym, where they showered and shampooed the little chunks of number two from their hair. They were out of school for the rest of the day.

The twins could know that my friends and I were behind the Great Baby Poop Balloon attack, but they couldn't prove it. I didn't even get called to the office by Mr. Chapman. See, everyone knew I was on the school bus with the twins that morning. How could I possibly have been responsible?

Weird, isn't it? I got blamed for the bug burritos, where I was the victim. But I didn't get blamed for the Great Baby Poop Balloon attack, where I was the mastermind. Like I said, there is no justice in fifth grade.

But the twins knew it was me. They knew it, all right. Which was cool, because there's no point in getting revenge if people don't know you've done it.

The only stupid thing I did was that I let my guard down. I mean, I figured it was all over. The twins had gotten us. And we'd gotten the twins back, good. I thought that was the end.

I was wrong.

They waited two days, just to make sure I was nice and relaxed. And then they struck.

I should have guessed something was coming, because that day at lunch the twins and Willie and Skank all brought lunch from home instead of eating cafeteria food. Even though the cafeteria had been opened again. And they were these really big bags of food. I never did see what they were eating, but there was a lot of it.

Anyway, that afternoon me and my friends were sitting in class, minding our own business and hurting no one. Mrs. Grady was blabbing away about something or other. The door opened and in comes Debbie. She shoots me this twisted little grin. And then she hands the teacher a note.

I felt my heart sink because I knew it had to be a note from the principal. Sure enough, Mrs. Grady read the note and then gave me a look like, "Oh, that Mark is always causing trouble."

"Mark Fine?" she said.

"Yes." I groaned.

"Mark Fine, Allie Hogan, Lester Peebles, and Zoner Russo, you will all go immediately to Mr. Chapman's office."

I thought, Uh-oh.

We all looked at each other and got up. Some kids whistled and made cute remarks like, "You guys are in TRUB-BULL."

Out in the hallway Zoner said, "What do you think this is about?"

"Duh," I said. "Take a guess. Why would Mr. Chapman ask the four of us to go to the office?"

"But you said he'd never be able to prove anything," Zoner whined.

I shrugged. "It was still worth it. No matter what Mr. Chapman does to us."

"Mark's right," Allie chimed in.

So we headed off down the hall, feeling nervous but also feeling good. Zoner was the first to spot it: a green rectangular piece of paper. It was just sitting there on the floor.

"Hey, that's money!" he said.

"That's a twenty-dollar bill," I agreed.

We both raced toward it. I mean, Zoner's my friend and all, but I wasn't just going to stand there and let him have the money.

We ran. Lester and Allie were right behind us.

Suddenly it was like a breeze picked up the money or something because it moved. If I had been thinking, I would have said, "Whoa, that money is moving. This has got to be a trap." But I wasn't thinking about anything except how cool it would be to have twenty bucks.

The money seemed to blow right across the hall toward an open door. It was the door to the janitor's closet. The money sort of hopped and skipped right in.

I piled into the closet. Zoner was right beside me. Allie plowed into my back, and Lester stumbled against her.

I snatched for the money and caught it. Then I realized there was a string attached to the money.

Right then, alarm bells kind of went off in my head. But it was too late. Suddenly someone slammed the closet door shut. It was pitch-black.

"Get that door!" I roared.

Lester snatched at the doorknob. I could hear from the way he was rattling it that the door was locked.

It was dark in the closet and so cramped that the four of us were all pressed in close to each other. I could barely turn around. And there were dirty mops and pails and cleaning supplies everywhere.

"It's a trap!" Lester said.

"No kidding," I said.

Just then a light appeared. It was a small, round hole, maybe as big as a baseball. Someone had cut the hole in the wall, fairly low down. It was just a couple of feet above the floor.

I tried to think—where did that hole lead to? What was on the other side of that wall? Then I realized it was the boys' bathroom.

I had a bad feeling about this.

"Well, well, well, well," a voice said. I recognized the voice. It was Darren Chapman. And his voice was coming through the hole. "Look what we have here. Four losers trapped in a closet. And the only fresh air comes through this little hole."

"Darren, you little creep. Let us out of here!" Allie yelled.

45

"I don't think so," a second voice answered. Debbie. I was a little surprised that Debbie would be in the boys' room. I managed to scrunch down and get my eye close to the hole. I could see the four of them—the twins, Skank, and Willie, all leering and laughing.

"Okay, big joke," I said, trying not to sound scared. "Let us out now. Let us out or I'm keeping this money!"

"Ha!" Debbie laughed. "The money's fake, you moron. Just like the note from my father."

"Debbie. Darren. Let us OUT!"

"Oh, no, no, no," Darren said. "The fun hasn't even started yet."

"That's right," Debbie agreed. "Do you know what we all had for lunch today?"

"Why would I care?" I asked.

"Beans," Debbie said. "Beeeeans," she repeated, drawing the word out slowly. "We each ate two cans of beans. And deviled eggs. And for breakfast we had bran muffins. But mostly we had beeeeans."

Cold fear gripped me. Beans. The four of them were loaded up with beans.

"Not laughing now, are you, Mark?" Darren said. He cackled his evil cackle and Debbie joined in.

I stared through the hole, horrified. Darren had turned away. He bent over, with his skinny hinder pointed right at me. Then, slowly, he backed up. He backed up until the hole went dark.

It started as a squeezer, making a sound like a party horn. Then it blossomed into a full-force farticane.

I reeled back as far as I could, but it wasn't far enough. I felt the foul wind on my face. The force of his flatus ruffled my hair.

"No!" Zoner screamed.

"Don't panic!" I cried. But the poopfume was already wafting toward our noses.

"Ugh! Ugh!" Allie cried. "It's . . . it's . . . it's HORRIBLE!"

"No more, no more!" Zoner yelled.

But there was no mercy. No mercy for any of us. This time the sound was no sound louder than a whisper.

"It's a silent killer!" I yelled. "Don't breathe! Cover your nose! It's a ninja fart!"

SEVEN

"Let us OUT!" I yelled.

"Someone save us! SAVE US!" Allie cried.

We were trapped in a world of stench. We screamed and cried and threatened, but no one rescued us.

One after another Darren and Debbie and Willie lined up to that one small opening and vaporized us. Whiff after whiff. Squeezers, poppers, multipoppers. Every kind of under thunder known to humankind. It was a reeking, stifling, gag-inducing nightmare.

And even when Darren, Debbie, and Willie had worn out their beans it didn't stop. They had kids lined up in the boys' room. The twins were paying a dollar to any kid who could fire a flatus.

We were hit again and again, fart after fart. Maybe a hundred farts, and all that nauseating stench locked in that one tiny closet with us.

Allie was the first to go. Someone unloaded a silent killer that smelled like something that had died a week ago. She passed out. Boom, down on the floor.

"Allie! Don't give up," I said, but it was too late. She was out cold.

"I . . . I can't take it anymore, Mark," Zoner said, moaning. "I can't hang on."

"You have to," I said. "We can't let them win. Do you hear me? We can't let them win!"

But Zoner's eyes rolled up in his head, and down he went in a heap.

It was down to me and good old Lester. Lester didn't even seem very upset. He was a rock.

"You still alive in there, Mark?" Darren asked.

"You'll never get me!" I cried. "I'm too tough for you. Me and Lester. We're both still standing. Do you hear me? We're still standing!"

"Not for long," Darren said.

I could tell from the sound of his voice that it wasn't just an empty threat. I knew he had saved up some final, secret weapon.

It had to be Skank.

"We've got one more for you, Mark," Debbie said. "This is more than just beans. More than just deviled eggs and bran muffins. We've been preparing this one since yesterday."

"You're not scaring me," I yelled back. Of course that was a lie. I was plenty scared.

"We added special ingredients for this whiff," Darren said. "Cabbage. Eggplant. And . . ."

Please, don't let him say blue cheese, I prayed silently.

"And . . . blue cheese!" Darren said. "Let him have it, Skank!"

Seconds later there came a whiff like nothing I'd experienced before.

"F-f-f-pop-pop-f-f-pop-f-f-pl-pl-pl-pl-pop-f-f-f-f-th-th-th-pop—"

It was like it was never going to end. It was the whiff of your worst nightmares. She could have peeled paint with that stench.

"F-pl-pl-pl-pop-f-f-squeeeeeze-popopopop-f-f-f—"

I clutched at my throat. My eyes watered.

My ears started ringing. My knees wobbled. I saw visions of my great-grandmother, who had died when I was little. She was far at the end of a long tunnel of light. She was waving to me.

"Put-put-f-f-f-BLAT-BLAT-f-f-f-f-shhhhh-pop-BLAAAAAAT—"

I felt Lester's hands trying to hold me up. But down I went. Down, down, down into blessed unconsciousness.

Unfortunately I came to around ten minutes later. It was right around then that Miss Featherstone, one of the teachers, found out what was going on. She unlocked the door. Inside she saw three of us crumpled on the floor. Only Lester was still standing.

The concentrated stench came blowing out in a huge blast of reek, and Miss Featherstone caught it all.

She quit teaching that same day. Later I heard she joined a cult.

They say war is hell. And now I know they're right.

For days afterward, there were the nightmares. I'd wake up suddenly in the middle of the night and man, it was like I was back there. Back in that closet, hearing the under thunder. Smelling the reek.

Or else I'd be just walking down the street and suddenly a car exhaust would *pop!* and I would panic. I'd try and hold my breath until I realized no, I wasn't back in the closet, man. It was just a car with a bad muffler.

Then there was my growing need for aftershave. Aftershave, cologne, even my mom's perfume. I'm not proud of it. I managed to get over it with some help. But it took time before I could go a whole day without splashing on some Old Spice.

Two days after the terrible Fart Closet Incident we all got together in the park. We were still a little shaky about small, smelly places. And my room always has a little of that old-socks smell.

"Hey, guys," I said.

"Hey, man, how's it going?" Zoner asked.

"It's been rough," I said. But then I clenched my jaw and said, "I'm cool now. And I'm ready for a little payback."

Allie looked troubled. "Mark, I don't know if I have the courage for this. I don't know if I can get back in the battle."

I gave her a confident grin. "Sure you can,"

I said. "Nobody can beat you. And look, soon we're all going to Adventure Land. Then we can put this war behind us."

She smiled back. "Yeah. You're right. We can't let the twins win."

"But what can we do?" Zoner asked.

I shrugged. "I don't know."

"You know . . . the twins are having a birthday party tomorrow," Lester said.

"How do you know that?" I asked him.

He looked embarrassed. "I heard about it."

"Heard about it from who?" I demanded.

Lester shrugged. "I happened to hear Sara . . . I mean, Skank . . . say something about it."

Zoner and Allie and I all circled around him. We were feeling mighty suspicious. "What exactly were you doing talking to Skank?" Allie asked.

"I was . . . I was . . . spying! That's it, I was spying. And see, I found out about the party, and that's good, right?" Lester said.

"Yeah, right," Zoner said. "Spying."

Lester was sweating. And I don't think any of us really believed him. But we couldn't afford to have conflicts in the group. Not when we were in a war. So I let it go.

"The party is a good thing," I said. "It's a

good opportunity to hit them when they aren't expecting it."

"Yes, but hit them with what?" Zoner said. "They got us with roaches. We got them with baby substance. Then they got us back with megawhiff. What's left?"

For a long time we just stood around, looking blank. A lady came by with her dog on a leash. The dog stopped a few feet away and took a dump.

Then Allie started laughing. She was watching the dog. And she was laughing an evil laugh.

"What?" I asked her.

She grinned. "The Chapmans have a swimming pool, right?"

EIGHT

The Chapman twins' birthday party started about two in the afternoon. But by that time me and Allie and Zoner and Lester had already spent hours in careful preparation. We had crisscrossed the park, armed with rubber gloves and plastic bags. We had purchased two large cans of Crisco shortening. We had swiped some panty hose from Zoner's big sister.

And we had drunk huge amounts of iced tea and water, and now our Super Soaker water guns were loaded. Only, not with water.

We hid behind some shrubs across the street from the Chapman house. I slung my Super-Soaker onto my shoulder. I raised my binoculars to my eyes and took a good, long look.

"Almost everyone is in the pool," I reported.

It was one of those aboveground pools. The sides looked about four feet high. There was a narrow wooden deck around the sides.

"There's Darren," I said. I focused the binoculars on him. He was standing on the deck in his bathing suit. "Go ahead, Darren," I whispered. "Jump on in."

"We can't do it unless both the twins are in the pool," Allie said.

"Agreed. And it would be nice to have Skank and Willie in there, too."

Darren refused to go in, though. It was starting to worry me. Maybe he was afraid of the water or something. Also the contents of our plastic bags were starting to get kind of ripe.

And with the sun beating down on us the Crisco was getting mushy.

"There he goes!" I cried. "Darren is in the pool!" I put down the binoculars. "All right. Just like we rehearsed. Panty hose, ON!"

We each had a single panty hose leg. We now pulled them on over our heads and down over our faces. They smushed our features and made us harder to recognize. I did a quick adult check. I didn't see any. If Mr. Chapman was there, he was well hidden. We would just have to take our chances. No guts, no glory.

"Allie? Zoner? Ready with Crisco?"

They both nodded and removed the plastic lids of their Crisco cans.

"Okay, and Lester and I are ready with the bags," I said. "Okay. Everyone PUMP UP!"

We all began pumping our Super Soakers.

"I'm pumped!" Zoner cried when his water gun was at full power.

I looked around at my friends. It almost gave me a little lump in my throat to see the brave looks on their faces. Although their faces looked squished in the panty hose.

"Remember the Fart Closet!" I cried. "Now, let's go get some PAYBACK!"

We ran across the street. The partyers were either in the pool or on the lawn around the pool. Most of them never even saw us coming. Or if they did see us, they didn't know how scared they should be.

We achieved almost total surprise.

"Crisco!" I cried.

Instantly Allie and Zoner ran to opposite sides of the aboveground pool. Each of them dipped a hand into the white grease. Then they smeared the shortening on the top edge of the pool. Allie is shorter, so she took the area where there was no deck. Zoner is pretty tall, so he was able to reach over the narrow wood deck to grease the rim.

A big kid I didn't know was coming toward us across the lawn. Maybe he was supposed to be in charge. Maybe he thought he was supervising. I don't know. All I know is he picked a real bad day to play babysitter. "Hey, what's going on?" he demanded. "What are they doing?"

"None of your business," I snapped.

"Hey, you little punk, don't tell me what's my business," the kid said. "I'll kick your butt."

"Oh, yeah?" I asked. I whipped the Super Soaker into firing position. "One move and I let you have it."

He snorted. "Like I'm terrified of a water gun? I'm already wet."

"It's not a water gun," I said. "It's a used water gun, if you get what I'm saying."

"Used water? What's used water?" It took him a couple of seconds to figure it out. "You have number one in that gun?"

"That's right, pal," I snapped. "Number one. Yellow stain. Squirt. The old warm and wet. Piddle. The letter that's missing between *o* and *q*. And unless you want a face load . . ."

"No problem, man," he said, quickly backing off. "None of my business."

Meanwhile Allie and Zoner had completed their task. I checked my watch: fifteen seconds. Better than we rehearsed. But naturally more and more of the kids in the pool had started to notice that something was going on.

"What is this stuff?" Willie yelled. I saw him, up to his neck in the water. He was gingerly touching the Crisco. It was easy to see that he was getting suspicious.

I ran around the side of the pool and climbed up onto the deck. What a sight! There were about twenty-five kids in the pool, including the twins, Skank, and Willie. It was pretty crowded in there.

"Who the . . . ?" Debbie yelled, looking up at me.

Some kid tried to climb out of the pool. She didn't make it. She tried to hoist herself up, but the Crisco worked perfectly. Her hands slipped off the greased rim and she fell back into the water.

"What is going on here?" Darren demanded. "Is that . . . Is that Mark Fine?"

I just stood there, enjoying the fear in his eyes. He couldn't see my face clearly because it was smushed by the panty hose. But I knew he was beginning to suspect.

Slowly I opened the plastic bag I was carrying. I reached inside with one gloved hand. And slowly I lifted out one of the dog sausages we'd picked up in the park. I held it out for all to see. All twenty-five kids in the pool fell totally silent. They just stared in horror.

"He's got a turd!" someone screamed suddenly.

I tossed the doggie flop up in the air. It spun and spun, like a baton thrown by a cheerleader. It almost seemed to hang in the air. Then it plummeted. Straight down. Down till it hit the water with a splash.

What followed was a joy to behold. It was total panic. There were screams! There were cries! People were clawing over each other, desperate to get away.

The dog log splashed, sank, then bobbed right back up to the surface.

That's a little known fact about a well-aged doggie sausage: it'll usually float.

"*Ahhhhhh!*" they cried. "*Noooooo!* Don't let it touch me! Get out of my way!"

And they all tried to scramble up out of the pool. They grabbed the sides and tried to hoist themselves up. But their hands slipped on the Crisco, and one by one they fell back in the water.

I caught Lester's eye. He was on the far side of the pool. He seemed to be looking at Skank, when he should have been watching me for the signal. "Hey, doofus," I yelled. He looked over and I said "Now!"

Lester opened his bag. I opened mine. We both turned them over. Out fell flotsam and jetsam of the canine variety. Not one or two but dozens of Lassie loaves. Twenty or thirty Beethoven movements. Maybe a hundred Benji bars.

"*Noooo!* It can't *beeeee*!" the kids cried. "Help us! HELP US!"

In the middle of the pool Debbie wailed, "Oh, oh, oh! Oh, the humanity!"

Kids were crying. Some were praying. But mostly they were just rushing around insanely. Terrified of touching the substance. But there was too much of it. Touching was going on everywhere. Some of the logs were submarining. Some had already sunk to the floor of the pool and were being crushed underfoot.

Others were being smashed between bare, panicked bodies.

The kids were churning the water so much the pool looked like a Jacuzzi.

"I'll get you for this!" Darren screamed. He was shaking his fist at me.

I was a little worried that adults might hear all the yelling and come out of the house. And let's face it, the adult in question was Mr. Chapman. I didn't want to have Mr. Chapman actually catch me there.

Also, I saw something that disgusted and frightened me. It was Skank.

Skank had remained cool through the whole thing. And now, she was busy licking the Crisco from one part of the pool rim. She was eating the Crisco! In a few seconds she would lick an escape route for the kids in the pool.

You had to admire her guts. I wished we had her on our side.

"Enjoy your party," I said to Darren, and gave a little wave. "You too, Debbie."

We retreated to safety. Two kids made it out of the pool, climbing up where Skank had slurped the shortening. They came after me. But the four of us caught them in a Super

Soaker yellow stain crossfire. They never had a chance.

As we ran we heard the voice of Mr. Chapman yelling, "Come BACK here, you little MONSTERS!"

But we little monsters were outta there.

NINE

Mr. Chapman couldn't do anything to me until I was back in school. Which I was the next day. And then he moved very fast.

I had barely rested my end zone in my desk seat when the announcement came over the public address: Mark Fine was to report to the office. IMMEDIATELY.

Everyone laughed, of course. Except my buds. Allie gave me an encouraging wink. But as I left the room I noticed that Darren and Debbie weren't in the room, either.

I found them in their father's office. They were sitting side by side, with their "perfect-little-sweetheart" looks plastered on their pasty faces. Mr. Chapman was looking slightly annoyed.

Actually he looked like he could basically chew his own desk and swallow it. The man was not happy.

"Hi, Mr. Chapman," I said in a phony happy voice. "Hi, Darren and Debbie. How's it going?"

Darren kept the same sappy look on his face, but I heard a low growl come from Debbie. And Darren's eyes had a definite dangerous look.

I swallowed hard and took a seat.

"Let's cut straight to the point here, Mark," Mr. Chapman said. "Someone filled my pool with dog feces. THAT SOMEONE IS YOU!"

I jumped a couple of feet straight up when he yelled. "Someone put dog doo in your pool?" I said. I tried hard to sound innocent. "Why do you think I did it?"

Mr. Chapman narrowed his eyes. "We KNOW you did it, Mark. We know. Darren and Debbie say you did it. You and your cretinous friends."

I thought, Hmmm, *cretinous*. That sounded like a cool word. I'd have to look it up.

"No way, Mr. Chapman. I am totally innocent. And so are my cretinous friends."

"Ha!" Debbie snapped. "Innocent? Yeah, right."

65

"You TOTALLY ruined our party," Darren said.

"You totally ruined my POOL!" Mr. Chapman said. "I have to have it DRAINED now. COMPLETELY drained and cleaned."

"I don't even know what you're talking about," I protested. "Why would I want to put dog dumplings in your pool?"

"For revenge," Debbie snapped.

I grinned. "Ohhhh?" I said, drawing out the word. "Revenge for what?" Fine, let them tell their father all about the fart closet if they wanted to.

Debbie went pale. She looked at Darren. He shook his head no.

"I didn't mean to say revenge," Debbie said lamely.

I knew I had them both. They didn't want me telling their father about the fart closet. Or the bug burritos. And now that Debbie had stupidly said the word *revenge*, Mr. Chapman might even believe me.

Mr. Chapman looked confused. He sent a troubled look from his evil son to his evil daughter.

"I think maybe you guys made a mistake," I said. "You know, about it being me."

Darren was grinding his teeth. But he said, "Yeah, maybe you're right. It must have been someone else."

Mr. Chapman's mouth dropped open. "Are you telling me it wasn't Mark?"

"No, Daddy," Debbie said. "We made a mistake. It wasn't Mark."

Mr. Chapman shook his head. For a minute I thought he might actually apologize. But no. He just said, "All right, get out."

"Yes, sir," I said cheerfully. I was so relieved, I was almost skipping down the hall on my way back to class. I couldn't believe I had gotten away with it.

Darren and Debbie came up behind me just as I turned the corner.

"You think you're smart, don't you, Mark?" Debbie asked.

I pretended to think about it. "Why, yes. Yes, I do. I doo. I dog doo all in your pool. Good luck ever getting anyone to have a pool party at your house again."

They just stood there giving me hate looks for a few minutes. Then they exchanged a glance. Darren said, "We have a proposal."

"A proposal?" I repeated. "Hmmm. What kind of a proposal?"

"This war is getting ugly," Darren said. "If it keeps up, something bad could happen."

"Yeah," I agreed. "Like, for example, your father could finally figure out what a couple of creepazoid, scumslithering monsters you really are."

Darren and Debbie both nodded. "Exactly."

You had to admit: they knew what they were.

"But you'll get in trouble, too," Debbie pointed out. "My dad hates your guts. He's just looking for an excuse to suspend you or even expel you."

I nodded. It was true. And that would be a drag. I didn't want to have to explain to my folks that I got expelled for making water balloons filled with my little sister's diaper gravy. Or for filling the principal's pool with dog poop.

Nothing good was going to come from that kind of conversation.

"All right," I said. "I'm listening. What's your proposal?"

Debbie looked over her shoulder, checking to make sure no one else was listening. "Here's the idea: single combat. You pick your best person. Your champion. We pick our best person. Our champion. It's a battle of the gross-outs. The first one to heave loses."

Darren explained further. "If your person spews first, then we win. Then you have to admit, in front of everyone, that we rule and that you drool."

I nodded thoughtfully. "I like it. I must admit, I like it. And I have an extra suggestion: we have the shoot-out on Friday when we take the field trip to Adventure Land."

I think the twins were impressed by my suggestion. "Good," Debbie said. "The combination of gross-out and sickening rides will be perfect."

"I assume you'll be choosing Lester as your champion," Darren said.

"You assume right," I said. "Lester will kick Willie's butt."

"Willie?" Darren laughed. "Willie won't be our champion. He's good, but he's not good enough to face Lester. Oh, no. Our champion will be Skank."

It rocked me, I can tell you. I felt my knees shake.

Skank!

I couldn't believe it. I had fallen victim to sexist stereotypes. I had assumed they would

69

choose a guy as champion. I was . . . politically incorrect.

I remembered the image of Skank slurping her way to freedom by gobbling up raw Crisco. I recalled the way she had been indifferent even as my little sister's diaper gravy dribbled down her face. And I could still smell that poopfume of hers.

Could even mighty Lester outgross Skank?

Suddenly I was afraid. I was very, very afraid.

TEN

"Atten-TION!" I snapped.

Lester looked surprised. He actually stopped scratching his rift. The four of us were in my room. I had put the sign on my door that said Do Not Disturb. My mom and dad usually respect my privacy. I think they're a little afraid of what they might see if they just barged into my room.

"All right, Lester," I said. "Stand up straight. Feet together. Shoulders back. Chest out. Suck that stomach in, misTER!" I stood with my hands clasped behind my back, inspecting our champion.

"As of this minute you are in training," I told him.

"In training? What's that?"

"He means like heavyweight boxers," Zoner explained. "You know, how they exercise and all before a fight. They work out with weights and stuff."

"Weights?" Lester moaned. "I have to lift weights?"

"No, no, no. It's not that kind of a battle," I reassured him. "But you still have to train. I know you have a strong stomach now, Lester. But we're going to make you even stronger, even better. We have the technology. We're going to make you one hundred percent heave-proof."

"I'm already—," he started to say.

Allie jumped up. "Don't argue, Lester. You're not just fighting for yourself, you know. You're representing all of us." She took him by the arm and looked right in his eyes. "You are our champion. Our CHAMPION!"

He looked honored. Also confused.

"You see, Lester, this is an idea that goes back to the days of the Knights of the Round Table," Allie explained. "Instead of having total war, each side has chosen its bravest, strongest knight. That knight will go forth and do battle. Oh, the very thought gives me chills. It's so . . . literary."

Lester thought about this for a moment. "Okay," he said. "But who's the other knight? You know, the one I have to battle?"

Allie and Zoner and I all exchanged glances. I was a little worried about this part. I didn't want to do anything to shake Lester's confidence. Not at this early point.

But he had a right to know.

"It's Skank," I said.

His eyes went sort of cloudy. He gazed up at the ceiling, like he was looking at something far, far away. A slight smile played over his lips.

"You're not scared?" Zoner asked.

"Scared?" Lester shook his head slowly. "No, I'm not scared."

"Good man," I said enthusiastically. "Don't you worry. You'll wipe the floor with Skank. You're the best."

"The best," Zoner agreed.

"Okay, now," I said. "We begin the training. We have some videos for you to watch. The purpose of these is just to toughen you up a bit. We're going to make grossness seem like no big deal. Just have a seat in front of the TV."

Lester sat down on my one and only chair. I

73

grabbed the remote control and hit Play.

"Okay, for a start I have tapes of that educational TV show where they do the operations on people. A full hour of guts. Guts and more guts. With lots of close-ups."

"That's cool," Lester said.

"Then we have Barney, Mister Rogers, and an entire John Tesh concert," I said.

Lester's face grew a little grim when he heard that.

"And finally we have a collection of commercials for false teeth goo, sanitary pads, old people diapers, diarrhea medicine, and—"

"Not the earwax removal system commercial!" Lester cried.

I put a comforting hand on his shoulder. He was trembling. "Yes, the earwax removal system commercial. I'm sorry, Lester, but this is training. It has to be tough. I know you're going to hate me for all I'm going to put you through. But I'm just trying to prepare you for battle. Later you'll thank me."

"We'll be downstairs," Allie said. "Call down when you're done with all the tapes."

"Oh, one more thing," I said. I walked over to my dirty clothes pile. I dug through the dirty sweat socks and the underwear. From

74

under the pile I pulled out an old, old bag of Fritos and a can of half-eaten bean dip.

"I think these Fritos have been under there since Christmas," I said. I handed them and the dip to Lester. The dip was crusty and growing a kind of cute white mold. "Those are in case you get hungry," I said. "And I expect to see them gone when I get back."

I felt bad leaving him that way. But it had to be done. He had to be in peak condition for the battle ahead.

For the rest of the week, every afternoon after school, we trained him hard. We put him through hell. We made him kiss his grandmother. We made him eat this low-fat casserole Zoner's mom made. We played Michael Bolton CDs. We had him swallow an entire giant bag of those bright orange circus peanuts and then feed my little sister her strained peas while we poked him in the stomach with hockey sticks.

We did everything we could to make him sick. But he never cracked.

Still, I knew we could never really prepare him. Let's face it, Lester was our friend. We couldn't do things as bad as the twins would do to him.

But Lester had natural talent. I had to hope that his natural talent, combined with the training, would enable him to win.

The night before the big day we all gathered one last time in my room. Allie wore a dress, and Zoner and I wore shirts with actual collars. It was kind of a big event.

I poured a glass of punch for everyone. When we each had a full glass, I said, "I want to drink a toast. So everyone raise your glasses."

Everyone did raise their glasses.

"A toast to Lester Peebles. Our classmate. Our friend. Our champion. Hurray for Lester!"

"Hurray for Lester!" Zoner and Allie cried.

Then Lester, Allie, and Zoner drank half their punch in a single long swallow. I didn't touch mine.

"One last test, Lester, before you graduate," I said. "I have to tell you something."

"What?"

"I peed in the punch."

"*Gaaahh-g-g-g!*" Allie said.

"*Bluh, bluh,*" Zoner said. "*Bluh.*"

I could see they were both getting ready to spew. I grabbed my trash can and handed it to Allie.

"If you have to heave, do it in there," I said. I looked curiously at Lester. He wasn't ready to spew.

Lester just smiled. He took a second big swig of the punch. He swirled it around in his mouth. He looked thoughtful. Then he swallowed.

"No way, Mark," he said. "You didn't pee in the punch. I would have tasted it."

The truth came too late for Allie and Zoner, who had their heads together and were chucking violently into my trash can. In between heaves they were muttering some pretty cruel words at me.

I felt so proud of Lester at that moment. He was a true champion.

"Congratulations, my friend," I told him. "You graduate from the training course with straight A's."

"Cool," he said.

Suddenly, as she was bent over the vomit bucket, Allie's glasses slid off her face and sank into the steaming, reeking gumbo.

"*Ohhhh,*" she wailed. "My glasses! They're covered with stomach contents!"

"No problem," Lester said. He swaggered over, full of his new confidence. "I'll dig those out for you."

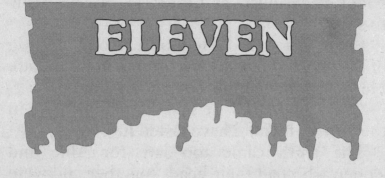

ELEVEN

awn seemed to come early that fateful morning. I awoke in the gray light, knowing that this day would be the most important day of my life.

I loaded my pockets with every kind of stomach medicine I could find: Tums, Pepto-Bismol, milk of magnesia. I figured they were my secret advantage. If it got to the point where I thought Lester might hurl, I would pour some of the pink stuff down his throat.

I refused to have any breakfast. No food, no barf. That's a scientific fact.

Then I went down to the school bus. I saw the twins, already sitting in their usual seats. They looked as grim as I felt. I gave them a nod. They nodded back.

Allie, Zoner, and our champion, Lester, were all sitting in the back of the bus. Zoner gave me a high five. Allie gave me a thumbs-up.

"How's it going, Lester?" I asked.

He gave me a confident smile. "I'm ready, Mark. I'm ready."

They dropped us at school and made us all get off the bus. Then they took roll and made us all get right back on the bus, only arranged by class. The usual dumb school stuff.

We were all sitting there, getting kind of excited because the next stop was Adventure Land. Kids were starting to play around. Throwing stuff and yelling and having a good time.

Then HE got on the bus.

Mr. Chapman.

That put an end to everyone having fun. We all stared at him. He wasn't wearing his usual business suit. He was wearing shorts. He was not a man who should ever wear shorts out in public.

I think we were all a little horrified and sickened by the sight of our principal's hairy legs. But far worse was what he said.

"Everyone, can I have your attention?" he

said. "I am going to be the chaperon for this group."

No one exactly burst out in applause. Not even the twins. Mr. Chapman was going with us? What kind of a cruel joke was this?

"You will be neat and orderly at all times," Mr. Chapman said. "No running. No chasing around. No yelling. No screaming. No fighting. No horseplay on any of the rides. No littering. No cutting in lines."

I thought, Great. Maybe we should just stay in class.

"You will OBEY all rules in the park. You will OBEY my orders. And you will OBEY all Adventure Land employees."

"Even the guy in the Daffy Duck suit?" I asked.

Bad idea. I really should have just kept my mouth shut. Mr. Chapman glared at me. "I have my eye on you, Mark Fine," he said. "Oh, yes. I have my eye on you."

It took half an hour to get to Adventure Land. Then it took another half an hour to cross the parking lot and get through the front gate.

But at last we were in!

Me and my friends waited for the twins and

their friends by the first T-shirt stand. Skank had been on another bus, so they had to wait to hook up with her.

But soon we saw them coming across the hot concrete: Darren Chapman. Debbie Chapman. Willie Leroux. And in the middle, looking big and powerful and confident, Sara "Skank" McPhee.

"All right, let's rumble," I said to Darren.

"We're ready, losers," he said. "But first: hand over your Pepto-Bismol."

I was surprised. How did he know? I pulled the Pepto from my pocket. And the Tums. And the milk of magnesia. "Okay," I said. "Now let's have yours. The only way you'd know I had that stuff is if YOU had some, too."

Darren smiled grimly. He snapped his fingers, and Willie began to unload their supply of stomach medicines. We dumped it all in the trash.

"Now, on to the rules," I said. "Our champion is Lester. Your champion is Skank. The goal is to make the other guy's champion barf. Whoever barfs first loses."

"That's right," Debbie agreed. "And we can do anything to make them hurl."

"As long as it isn't illegal or fatal," I agreed.

"If we tell your champion to do something and he refuses, then you guys lose. So long as our champion is willing to do it. Right?" Darren said.

I nodded. "I think we all understand the rules of this game." I leaned close, getting right in his face. "Let's get it ON!"

"You are going DOWN!" Darren sneered.

"Prepare to suffer TOTAL defeat!" I said.

"You're MINE, loser," Darren shot back.

Out of the corner of my eye I saw Lester smile at Skank. "Isn't this fun?" he said.

"I've never been a champion before," Skank agreed.

"Okay," I said. "I think first we'd better see about some food. I think Lester may be hungry."

"Not as hungry as Skank," Debbie said.

Adventure Land is arranged in this kind of big loop, with rides on both sides of the path. And there were side paths leading to bathrooms and to boring stuff that no one wanted to do. Like all this stuff about how to make cartoons.

Mostly they have all kinds of cool rides at Adventure Land. You know how some amusement parks are full of all that crafts stuff? Or else educational things about foreign countries? Well, fortunately there isn't much of that at Adventure Land.

Normally I would have gone straight for the three big roller coasters. I love roller coasters. But we had a mission. And first stop had to be the area where they sell food.

We marched as a group to the food area. There were stalls selling food all around us. Brightly painted signs advertised every great food item there was. The smell of mustard and grease was in the air.

"What first?" Debbie wondered.

"Cotton candy," Allie suggested.

So we trooped to the cotton candy stall. "We'd like . . . oh . . . twenty cotton candies," I said.

"Twenty?" the cotton candy lady asked. "But there are only eight of you kids."

"Twenty," I repeated. This battle was going to wipe out my allowance, and Allie's and Zoner's and Lester's, too. But wars are expensive.

We all stood there, holding these huge pink cotton candies. And then the two champions began to eat. At first Skank got out to a strong lead. She was half a candy ahead. But then Lester turned on the speed. By the seventh candy he got so he could just crush the whole thing into a big, sweet, sticky pink ball and shove it all in his mouth at once. Like swallowing a pink baseball.

"Go, go, go, Skank, go," Debbie urged.

"Yay, Lester, you're our man!" Allie cheered.

The two of them finished at the same moment. Watching them, I wondered if they would just barf right now. I mean, ten cotton candies?

"Liquid! We need some liquids!" Debbie said.

And so we all went over to the drink stand. Lester and Skank each poured down about a gallon of root beer.

Zoner pulled me aside. "You know, Mark," he whispered. "When one of them finally hurls, it's going to be dangerous."

"That's what we want," I said. "We don't want some little dribble of barf. When Skank blows, we want her to blow like Old Faithful."

So we loaded up our two champions. We stuffed them with everything we could find. In addition to the ten cotton candies each and the gallon of root beer, each champion swallowed six candy apples, including seeds. A dozen fully loaded chili dogs, plus six corn dogs with mustard. Nine DoveBars. Ten big soft pretzels. Three large bags of caramel corn. Lemonade. Hamburgers. Tacos. And some of those pellets you feed to the animals in the petting zoo.

Darren and I looked at each other. I think we were both a little worried.

But neither of us could show it. I put on my coolest grin and said, "All right. Let's see how tough your girl really is. It's time. It's time . . . to RIDE!"

TWELVE

Lester and Skank almost waddled toward the first roller coaster. I mean, you could tell they were full. Their stomachs were hanging over their belts. Their pants were bulging. They looked like overinflated water balloons ready to pop.

"How should we do this?" Allie wondered as we lined up for the first coaster.

"What do you mean?" I asked her.

"I mean, should we sit in front of Lester and Skank or behind? If we sit in front and they heave during a slow part of the ride, we'll get stomach contents all over us. But if they launch during a fast part, when the wind is whipping past, and we're behind them . . ."

I nodded. "Yeah, I see the problem." I

sighed. No matter how much you try and plan, there's always some problem you don't expect. "I'm making a decision here," I announced. "I have to go with behind being better than in front. I hope I'm right."

The way it worked out, Darren, Debbie, and Willie sat toward the front. Then Lester and Skank—they were so bloated they took up all three seats. Then me, Allie, and Zoner.

We were praying for a forward barf. I guess the twins were praying just as hard for wind-whipped puke.

Isn't it cool right at the start of a roller coaster? You know, when you're all strapped in and there's that first jerk when the car starts to move? And then you go crank, crank, cranking up that first big hill? And you can look all around and see the whole amusement park, and you're really looking forward to that first incredible drop?

Well, it's not quite as cool when the whole time you're thinking, Please, please, please don't let me drown in a giant explosion of chewed-up, half-digested amusement park food.

We cranked to the top of the hill.

"How's it going, Lester?" I yelled out. We

topped the hill and went plunging down, down, DOWN.

"*Cooool!*" Lester cried.

"*Wheeeee!*" Skank shrieked.

"Please don't woof," I muttered. "And if you do, please let it hit the twins."

We hit the bottom of the hill and my stomach did the wiggle. Then we rattled into a sharp turn and my stomach lurched. Right away, a sudden turn to the right and a loop! Up we went, up and over, and I thought, No way they can keep all that food down!

But they did! Neither of them extruded.

"We're gonna make it!" I yelled to Allie and Zoner.

"But we WANT Skank to blow, right?" Zoner pointed out.

"Yeah," I agreed. "Just not right now."

Curve after curve. Loop after loop. Gut-wrenching drop after gut-wrenching drop. Nothing was emitted from either champion's gullet.

We all breathed a sigh of relief as the car coasted in to a stop.

"How you holding up, man?" I asked Lester.

"I feel full," Lester said, quietly so the others

couldn't hear. "I'm getting fartatious. I mean, big-time fartatious. I could fire an ejection seat right now. I've never felt so inflated. I could blow a hole in my pants. And I don't want to blow a hole in my pants. These are my favorite pants."

"You hold on," I said urgently. "Do NOT fire that popper. Do not fumigate till I tell you to fumigate." I saw an opportunity. I ran over to Darren and Debbie and Willie, who were all gathered around Skank.

"Hey," I said, trying to sound casual. "How about they do the Rocket to the Moon next?"

Darren looked suspicious. "That's just what I was going to suggest."

So off we went to the Rocket to the Moon. I didn't want to make Lester walk too fast because I was worried he might let some vapor out. You know how it is when you walk and you're feeling fartatious? You can get that uncontrolled poppage. And I wanted Lester to stay at full intensity.

But he was a champion, all right. He held on. Not even a puff.

The Rocket to the Moon ride is these little capsules on a big long arm. The capsules are enclosed all around except for this little screen thing you can see out of. Only two people fit inside each capsule. Then it gets swung around and around.

Normally I like the ride. But this time I was glad there was only room for two.

"Okay, guys," I said. "Lester and Skank, in you go. Um, Darren?" I asked innocently. "Would you like to try and squeeze in with them? It's fun."

But Darren isn't stupid. Rotten, yes, but not stupid.

They closed the door on the capsule, squishing Lester and Skank into the tight space. I crossed my fingers.

I pulled Allie and Zoner aside and whispered, "Lester is ready to fire the biggest fart of his life. I guess it's all that food we fed him. When he vaporizes in that closed space, it's sure to make Skank heave. Or it may kill her."

Allie grinned. Then she looked serious. "But Mark, if eating all that food inflated Lester, won't it do the same thing to Skank?"

My eyes went wide. Of COURSE! No wonder Darren and Debbie went along with taking them to the Rocket!

"Oh, no," I moaned. See, I had been on the receiving end of Skank's whiff. I knew how terrible it could be. My heart went out to Lester, all alone in there.

"I guess instead of calling it the Rocket to the MOON they should have called it the Rocket to URANUS!" Zoner said, then started giggling.

I gave him a dirty look. I don't approve of childish jokes.

The ride started up. The Rocket started to swing left and then swiftly climbed into the sky. Up it went, and over, and down, and around. Faster and faster and faster.

Then the ride reversed direction—you know, the way they do to make you good and sick? The Rocket capsule stopped at the top of its arc. For a frozen moment of time it hung there, high overhead.

Then a sudden explosion!

BOOM! It was like a bomb.

And then a second explosion! *BOOM!* Just as loud as the first.

The capsule rattled and shook from the impact.

"Oh, no!" Debbie cried. "No! They both whiffed! Simultaneous buttal explosion!"

"Get them down!" I screamed at the ride operator. "Get them down, right now!"

THIRTEEN

The Rocket came to a stop. The ride guy opened the door. Immediately he fell to the ground. I guess he tried to breathe, and that was a mistake.

I rushed forward to try and help Lester and Skank climb down, but I hit a wall of stench that made my knees turn to jelly. I backed up real quick.

Lester and Skank climbed down. They looked a little sick. They looked a little green. But I peered at their stomachs: no wave motion. I stared at their throats: no signs of the gack dance.

"They didn't chuck!" Debbie said in an awed tone of voice.

"Neither of them blew," Allie said. "I can't believe it!"

The ride attendant was just starting to wake up. I think he was okay. Not actually dead or anything.

"Incredible," Darren said. "After all they ate? On that ride? Totally stenched? And neither of them heaves?"

"It's a miracle," Zoner said.

"Yeah, but we have to have a winner," Darren said. "Either that or it's back to all-out total war."

I nodded. "For the sake of peace, we have to have an answer," I agreed. "One of them must launch their lunch. We must have a hurl."

"All I can think is we need more food," Darren said. He seemed as puzzled as I was. I guess ordinary people are always a little puzzled when they see a miracle.

"More food," I agreed.

We headed back to the food area. It was my turn to buy again. And I was just about out of money. I laid out my last few dollars to buy two large chocolate milk shakes. I handed one each to the champions.

"Wait!" Willie said. For the first time he was getting involved. It made me worry.

He took the two milk shakes and set them on the counter. Then he turned around. He

93

pointed at his face. "I have two big zits," he said.

"You ARE a big zit, Willie," I said.

He ignored me. "I'll pop one in each milk shake."

I swear just hearing him say that almost made me blow chunks, but since I hadn't eaten anything I was chunkless. Even Lester thought this was gross. But I could see determination in his eyes.

Willie did it. I wanted to turn away. But you know how it is when something totally awful is happening? It's hard not to watch.

Willie leaned close, putting his greasy Klingon face right up over the first milk shake. Then with two fingers he volcanoed the first zit. Right into the milk shake.

After the first one I didn't feel like I had to watch the second time. Then Lester and Skank each took one cup.

"This is going to do it," I told Zoner and Allie. "No one can stand this. One of them is going to lose it."

The two of them sucked the milk shakes down in about a minute.

"I like strawberry better," Skank commented.

"You do?" Lester asked. "Me too."

We took them on the Tilt-A-Whirl.

We fed them funnel cakes.

We took them on the bumper cars.

We fed them onion rings.

We took them on a standing-up roller coaster.

We fed them nachos with extra cheese.

We took them on the water slide.

Nothing. There was no heavage. Neither of them extruded. There were no guttal explosions. The twins and Willie on their side and me, Zoner, and Allie for our side were completely depressed.

We felt like failures. We were beaten.

Debbie started to cry at one point. And I heard Zoner sniffling, too. It's a sad thing to be in fifth grade and know that you're a loser. That you have failed at the most important thing you've ever tried.

"We have to . . . to . . . to try again," I said. But I wasn't very enthusiastic.

"Yeah," Darren agreed. "We can't give up. Can we?"

"If we give up, it will mean going back to total gross-out war," Allie said glumly.

"It could go on forever," Debbie said.

95

"We have to try again," Allie agreed. "All I am saying is, give peace a chance."

"Guys?" Zoner said.

"Yeah, Zone, what is it?" I asked.

"Well, I have an idea. It's kind of disgusting, though."

"Just KIND OF disgusting? We've done KIND OF disgusting. We need something so sickening that we can't even say it out loud without wanting to woof."

"I guess I have it," Zoner said quietly. "I was kind of crying . . . and you know when you cry, your nose runs, right?"

"Mine is running, too," Debbie said.

Zoner nodded solemnly. "Let's not even say it out loud. I'll do Skank. Debbie, you do Lester."

I . . . I can barely even bring myself to describe what happened next. And if you have a weak stomach, please, please, PLEASE stop reading now.

I'm warning you.

Okay. If you're still reading, then don't blame me, okay?

What happened next was that Zoner went to stand in front of Skank. And Debbie went to stand in front of Lester.

96

And Zoner took Skank's mouth and brought it down, almost like he was going to kiss her. Only instead of putting her lips on his, he put her mouth over his nose.

And at the same time Lester closed his mouth over Debbie's runny nose.

"On the count of three," Zoner said. "One! Two!"

I couldn't even breathe. Of course, neither could Zoner or Debbie.

"THREE!" Zoner yelled.

At the same moment Debbie and Zoner honked. They sneezed. They sucked in air through their mouths and unloaded again.

"K-khhhaak-khh!"

"Hhhuunnng-ghk!"

"Snnnnooooork!"

FOURTEEN

We all piled back on the bus at the end of the day. Most of the kids were laughing and telling jokes and having a good time. At least until Mr. Chapman got back on the bus.

But me and my friends, and the twins and Willie, just sat silent. There was nothing more to say. Lester and Skank had not heaved. Not even the snotter had made them hurl.

The two of them were sitting side by side toward the front of the bus. They were both totally swollen with food. But they looked happy.

I guess it's a good thing to be able to stay happy in the middle of a disaster.

The bus started up and we headed back to town.

Mr. Chapman got up and came back to look at me. "What's the matter with you?" he demanded.

I shrugged. "Nothing, Mr. Chapman."

"You seem . . . quiet. Calm. Almost . . . normal," he said. He was obviously suspicious. But I didn't care. I didn't care about anything. I was a loser.

Mr. Chapman turned to his own kids. "And what's with you two?" he asked. "Didn't you have fun?"

They nodded in glum unison. "Sure. Lots of fun, Dad."

Mr. Chapman looked puzzled. He shook his head and went back to sit down right in front of Lester and Skank.

Lester and Skank were whispering. And I had the weird feeling that they were holding hands or something. Lester is a year older than me, but still, that was no excuse for holding hands with a girl.

We rode along in silence. But more and more I looked at Lester and Skank. I'm telling you: they were holding HANDS! It was sad to see. It kind of made me mad. I mean, they were our champions, right? They weren't supposed to like each other.

"This is grinding my nerves," I muttered to Allie.

"Why?" she demanded.

"It just IS," I said.

"I think it's sweet," Allie said.

The way she said it made me squirm. I don't know why. I got up and started to go forward. I wanted to see if it was true. I wanted to see with my own eyes whether MY champion was holding hands with the ENEMY!

But as I got to their seat, I saw something even worse.

Skank suddenly leaned very close to Lester.

"No WAY!" I yelled.

But it was too late. Skank's lips touched Lester's lips.

A kiss had occurred. Right there in front of me.

Lester and Skank both pulled back suddenly.

"Oh!" Skank cried.

"Whoa!" Lester said.

I saw Skank swallow hard. Then Lester did the same. Their faces were bright red. Their eyes bulged.

Was it love or something? I narrowed my eyes and looked hard at them. Then I saw it:

100

the first ripples in their bloated stomachs. The squeezing of their throat muscles.

It was the gack dance!

It was incredible. After all they had survived, it was the kiss that was going to make them heave.

I guess that tells you something about the power of love.

"They're gonna BLOW-W-W!" I cried.

The bus turned a corner too sharp and I lost my balance. I fell across their laps. I was looking up at their spazzing throats. I was seeing their lips writhe. I could feel their stomachs loading up to fire.

I scrambled up as fast as I could. "RUN!" I shouted. "RUN for your LIVES! They're gonna LAUNCH!"

Mr. Chapman jumped up and turned around. He put his hands on his hips and gave me a dirty look. Then he looked down at Lester and Skank, who were right behind him. I guess even Mr. Chapman knows the vomit look. His face went white.

I can't believe it, but I actually tried to save Mr. Chapman. Don't ask me why. But I yelled, "Mr. Chapman! RUN! RUUUUN!"

But it was too late.

101

"B-buub-bllleeeaaahhhh-kh-kh-kh!"

Lester and Skank blew at the same, exact time. The two vomit streams hit Mr. Chapman like a fire hose. The force of the guttal explosion knocked him back. He fought to stay on his feet, but—

"G-g-gugu-g-g-gov-v-BLEAH!"

A second round hit Mr. Chapman in the face. Down he went.

But Lester and Skank had barely even started. It was stomach contents everywhere. Puke in every color of the rainbow. Cotton candy barf and hot dog barf and funnel cake barf. It rolled down the aisle and I headed for higher ground. I stood on the seat as the tidal wave of heave rolled by.

Kids were screaming. The driver was screaming. Mr. Chapman was screaming.

It was great!

I pumped my fist in the air. "YES! YES! YES!"

"But who blew first? Who won?" Darren yelled to me just as the fourth or fifth explosion of puke emitted.

"Don't you get it?" I yelled back. "There are no losers. WE both won. We ALL won!"

Well, all except Mr. Chapman. I talked to

Darren and Debbie the other day. We're all buds now. They say Mr. Chapman is feeling much better now that they have him on stronger medication. No word yet on when he's coming back—if ever.

Glossary of Terms

barf: 1. *noun.* Matter ejected from the stomach through the mouth. 2. *verb.* To eject matter from the stomach through the mouth. Past tense: barfed.

Beethoven movements: *noun.* From the popular dog movies, meaning dog doo.

Benji bars: *noun.* From the less popular dog movies, meaning Beethoven movements.

blatt: 1. *noun.* A belch. 2. *verb.* To belch.

blow: *verb.* To throw up in a violent way. As in, *Look out, he's gonna blow chunks!*

brown substance: *noun.* Ordure.

buttal explosion: *noun.* A sudden, powerful, and loud fart.

buttal region: *noun.* The portion of the human body that is approximately halfway between the feet and the head and that is located on the rear side.

butt product: *noun.* Can also be written as *buttal product*.

chocolate log: *noun.* Brown substance in a neat, cylindrical form.

chuck: *verb.* To heave. To barf.

diaper gravy: *noun.* The brown substance commonly found in babies' diapers just moments after they were last changed.

dog log: *noun.* See *dog sausage*.

dog sausage: *noun.* See *dog log*.

ejection seat: *noun.* A condition that arises when a seated person pops a whiff so powerful that he is literally lifted out of his seat.

emit: *verb.* Past tense: emitted. To spew, gack, woof, or hurl.

end zone: *noun.* Buns. Hinder. Buttal region.

extrude: *verb.* To emit.

fartatious: *adjective.* The feeling of needing desperately to fire a flatus.

farticane: *noun.* From *hurricane*. A flatus so powerful that observers can actually feel the breeze from it.

flatuosity: *noun.* A talent for controlled or directed farting.

flatus: *noun.* Gas. Whiff. A fart.

flotsam and jetsam: *noun.* Usually refers to floating brown substance.

fumigate: *verb.* To fire a flatus. To pop a whiff. To vaporize.

gack: 1. *noun.* Vomit substance. As in, *There was gack everywhere.* 2. *verb.* As in, *She gacked up all over the place.*

gack dance: *noun.* The spasms observable in the throat of a person preparing to gack, blow, heave, hurl, or emit.

gumbo: *noun.* A thick and chunky vomit.

guttal: *adjective or adverb.* Refers to the stomach, or activities having to do with the stomach, or stomach products of all types.

guttal explosion: *noun.* A sudden powerful and unexpected gack, woof, hurl, barf, or puke.

heave: *verb.* To vomit.

hinder: (Rhymes with *finder.*) *noun.* Rear end. See also *buttal region.*

Lassie loaves: *noun.* From the popular TV dog, Lassie.

launch: *verb*. To vomit in a forceful or dramatic fashion. See also: *gack, heave, spew, emit*, and *extrude*.

matter: *noun*. Used generally to denote any of a number of bodily fluids. Synonym: *substance*.

morbific: *adjective*. Horrible, terrible, awful. As in, *Boy, those brussels sprouts are morbific*.

mucilage: *noun*. Snot.

multipopper: *noun*. A whiff that comes in a series of separate and distinct explosions.

ninja: *noun*. Silent or stealthy, also meaning very smooth.

ninja fart: *noun*. A flatus with the characteristics of ninja; i.e., a quiet, almost unnoticed flatus of great power.

nose noodle: *noun*. A hanging booger.

noxious: *adjective*. See *morbific*.

odious: *adjective.* Pretty much the same as *noxious.*

ordure: *noun.* Meaning brown substance.

poopfume: *noun.* Derived from the French *parfum.* The distinctive aroma of a flatus.

pooptonium: *noun.* One of the less well-known by-products of atomic research. See *brown substance.*

popper: *noun.* A fart that is expressed in a single, loud concussion.

puff: *noun.* A relatively harmless whiff.

reek: *noun.* A stench, an awful or unpleasant odor.

silent killer: *noun.* A type of flatus that makes no sound, thus striking by surprise and inflicting maximum psychological trauma.

snotsicles: *noun.* Frozen mucus extending down the upper lip from nostril to mouth.

snotter: *noun.* A nose noodle meant for human consumption.

spew: *verb.* To vomit.

squeezer: *noun.* A flatus that causes a horn-like or trumpetlike noise.

squirt: *noun.* Weewee.

stomach contents: *noun.* Puke.

substance: *noun.* In the general sense, meaning gross stuff of many kinds. See also *brown substance.*

under thunder: *noun.* The thunderlike sound of a flatus. As in, *He can really play that under thunder.*

used water: *noun.* See *squirt.*

vaporize: *verb.* To fire off a flatus.

vocals of vomit: *noun.* An idiomatic phrase referring to the characteristic gagging and groaning of a person preparing to blow chunks.

volcano: *verb.* To *volcano* is to squeeze a zit till it erupts.

vomitous: *adjective.* A type of object, person, or sensory impression that inclines an individual to heave.

whiff: 1. *noun.* A fart. 2. *verb.* To fart.

woof: *verb.* To vomit.

yellow stain: *noun.* Squirt. What's missing between *o* and *q*.

"No! You can't really mean it! Nooooooo!" I wailed. "Not summer camp!"

It was two hours later. I had almost gotten the reek off me. Almost. And I was looking forward to some peace in the safety of my room. But nooooo, that would be too easy.

"Dad, don't! Don't make me!" I cried.

But my father was no more impressed by my pathetic cries than that bully Hedley Hampton and his pals had been.

See, my dad is a marine. And not just any old marine—he's in some special parachute squad that jumps from airplanes and lands behind enemy lines. Except that they usually refuse to use the parachutes because that makes it too easy.

"Look, Robert," he said, "it's time for you to grow up. You are going, and that's all there is to it."

"But Dad, I can't go to summer camp! I won't know any of the kids there. I won't like the food. I won't be able to fall asleep in a strange bed. Remember the time I had to sleep at Grandma's and I was up all night? Do you want me to die from lack of REM?"

"Maybe we should reconsider, dear," my mother said. Good old mom. She's always on my side.

"We are *not* reconsidering," my dad said firmly. "We agreed. It's time to cut the apron strings. A boy needs to learn some independence if he's ever going to become a man."

"I don't want to be independent!" I whimpered. "I don't want to be a man!"

Yeah, I know. Pretty sickening, right? But at the time I was just terrified of the idea of camp. It was like regular life was bad enough, you know? And now my parents wanted to make it even worse.

"You leave next week, Robert. Next Saturday at oh nine hundred hours, to be precise. Nine A.M. You're going to Camp Winnapuke."

For the next week I tried every trick I knew to change their minds. I whined. I wept. I wheedled. I pretended I had cancer, measles, anything and everything. But then, the more I thought about pretending to be sick, the more I worried I would *really* get sick, which just made me nauseous.

So I gave up the deathbed approach. I went back to pleading for mercy. As the dreaded Saturday deadline crept closer, I pulled out all the stops. I squelched my last tiny shred of self-respect and just wallowed and groveled like a worm. But nothing worked.

The week passed. My parents bought me a notebook and some stamps so I could write them letters. I knew I was doomed.

Then it was Saturday.

My parents woke me up at seven thirty. I pretended I had lockjaw. I called out, "Help! I have lockjaw and I can't move my mouth!" but they didn't buy it. Then I tried mumbling some nonsense in a southern accent, claiming I'd contracted Forrest Gump syndrome. They didn't believe that, either. Then they packed my bags.

My mom was crying when I left. At least I

think she was. It was hard to tell over the sound of my own loud wailing.

My dad drove me to the place where the buses came to collect kids for camp. But just before we got there, he did something strange. He pulled over to the side of the road and turned off the engine.

"Son," he said.

"Yes?" I said hopefully. I thought, Okay, maybe he's changed his mind.

"Son, you know what I do for a living, right?"

"Sure."

"And you know I've got a lot of medals and stuff. Things that prove how brave and tough I am. Medals for heroism. Medals for getting hurt. Medals for that time I was behind enemy lines and had to live on nothing but worms and pig sweat."

I could feel my stomach starting to squirm. I hated that story about the worms and pig sweat. "Yeah, Dad," I said glumly. "I know you're brave and tough and nothing makes you sick. But I'm just not like you. I'm not brave and tough. I'm a coward. I can't eat worms. The very thought of it . . ."

"Roll down the window!" he yelled.

I rolled it down and stuck my head out. *"Bleah. Uuuug-g-g-BLEAH!"* I spewed out into the fresh morning air. It wasn't a huge spew. Just kind of a moderate extrusion.

"Are you done?" my dad asked.

I nodded. "Just don't tell any more war stories, okay?"

"I was trying to make a point, Robert. See, I know you think I'm this big, strong guy who can handle anything. But what you don't realize is that I used to be just like you."

I wiped a stray chunk of stomach contents from my lips. "You mean you were a weak-stomached coward?" I said bitterly.

"Exactly. A pathetic pusillanimous puker."

Good old Dad. He doesn't really believe in all that stuff about being supportive and positive to your kids.

"Where do you think you got those qualities?" my father asked. "You got them from *my* side of the family. You inherited them from me."

I was stunned. I couldn't believe that my dad would share this story with me. That he would trust me with his bittersweet story of geekhood. I felt suddenly really close to him.

So I said, "Does that mean I don't have to go to camp? Please, please, please, oh please?"

He rolled his eyes. "No, Robert. You're not listening. I'm telling you: I used to be just like you. Until one summer my dad made me go to summer camp. In fact, it was Camp Winnapuke. The same camp you're going to."

I looked at him suspiciously.

"See, son, it was my time at Camp Winnapuke that made me the man I am today. Before that I was a sniveling, gutless worm with a stomach so weak I used to woof up a kidney at the very mention of oysters."

I thought of what he was trying to say. Then I thought of oysters. All gray and slimy, like a glob of snot on the half shell. . . .

"Roll down the window!" my dad ordered.

When I was done, he looked me straight in the eyes. "Trust me on this. Camp Winnapuke will change the way you live your life." He smiled mysteriously. "You may find that by facing the thing you fear most—the most nauseating, sickening, disgusting thing in the world—you'll get to a place beyond fear, beyond even the urge to purge."

"So you're saying I still have to go?"

I was blubbering pretty good by the time the bus came. It was okay, though, because there were other kids crying, too. Of course they were all a couple of years younger.

But I was trying to stop my weeping because I was hoping that maybe . . . just maybe . . . my dad was right. Maybe camp would change everything. Maybe I would become a new kind of person. Maybe I would get all the other kids to like and respect me. Maybe . . .

Or maybe not.

I climbed on the bus. And then through my tears I saw something that made me twice as scared and three times as sick as I'd been up till then.

The something was sitting in the back of the bus: Hedley Hampton. And Jamal Ishiyama. And Buttfire Tisch. The worst bullies in school!

I could feel my stomach begin to squish like a water balloon. The countdown to the launch started. Ten . . . nine . . . eight . . .

It was an out-of-control gack dance!

Seven . . . six . . .

Stomach pressure at maximum!

I looked at the person in the seat beside me. It was a girl with red hair. She was kind of pretty.

"Window . . . ," I said in a low voice. "The window . . ."

She looked closely at me. "You look like you're ready to spew," she said.

I nodded. In my head the countdown was moving on, unstoppable!

Five . . . four . . . three . . .

Suddenly the girl grabbed the window. "Hold on!" she yelled. She tried to yank the window down, but it was stuck!

Two . . . one . . .

I gritted my teeth.

"No," the girl cried. "Don't vomitize me!"

Down came the window with a bang, but too late!

Blastoff!

I blew like a volcano. I was Mount Vomituvious. I was Pukatao.

My teeth were still gritted tightly. But it was no use. There's no stopping the force of nature.

Barf squirted through the cracks between my teeth. The force of it blew out a front tooth that was kind of loose anyway. The tooth flew through the air and landed in the girl's red hair.

Right behind it came hot stomach contents. They shot through the hole in my teeth like a fire hose. The spray hit the girl in the face.

Desperately I turned away, but I was like a squirting hose. The puke stream sprayed across the kids sitting in front of me.

"Oh, yagh! Yagh! Gross! YUCK!" they screamed.

In total panic I turned the other way and hosed the kids across the aisle.

"No! Get away from me! No! NOOO!"

The pressure let up. I swallowed all the vomit I could, but mostly it was spread all around me.

I surveyed the damage I had done. Sixteen kids had been hit by the guttal explosion. Their hair dripped with my chunks. My steaming gumbo slithered down their faces.

Then I realized there was someone standing over me: Hedley. Followed by Buttfire and Jamal. None of them had been hit.

"Well, well, well," Hedley said in a loud voice. "Up to your usual tricks, eh, Baby? Everyone, may I have your attention?"

He didn't need to get everyone's attention, trust me. They had already noticed me. Especially the kids I'd heaved all over.

"This is Baby Worm," Hedley said gleefully.

The dreaded nickname reverberated around

the bus. I could hear kids repeating it. "Baby Worm . . . Baby Worm."

The bus driver didn't seem to notice the hysteria and violent chucking. He was too busy flipping a floppy goober out of his nose. He put on the gas and started the bus.

I was on my way to camp. I was accompanied by three guys who enjoyed torturing me. And I had already blown breakfast all over everyone within range, which was not going to help me become popular.

So far the whole experience was turning out even worse than I had expected. And I wasn't even out of the parking lot yet.

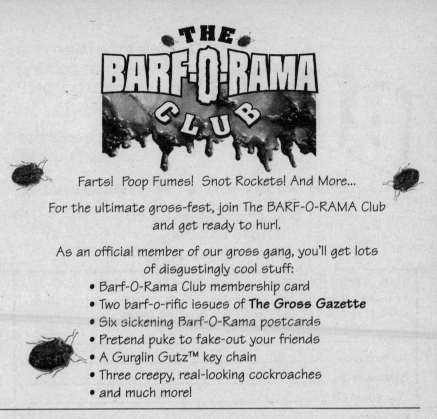

THE BARF-O-RAMA CLUB

Farts! Poop Fumes! Snot Rockets! And More...

For the ultimate gross-fest, join The BARF-O-RAMA Club and get ready to hurl.

As an official member of our gross gang, you'll get lots of disgustingly cool stuff:

- Barf-O-Rama Club membership card
- Two barf-o-rific issues of **The Gross Gazette**
- Six sickening Barf-O-Rama postcards
- Pretend puke to fake-out your friends
- A Gurglin Gutz™ key chain
- Three creepy, real-looking cockroaches
- and much more!

Join the BARF-O-RAMA Club for the one year membership fee of only $5.50 for U.S. residents, $7.50 for Canadian residents (U.S. currency). Includes shipping & handling.

Send a check or money order (do not send cash) made payable to "Bantam Doubleday Dell" along with this form to:

✂ -

BARF-O-RAMA Club, PO-Box 12393, Hauppauge, NY 11788

NAME _____

(Please print clearly)

ADDRESS _____

CITY _____ STATE _____ ZIP _____

(Required)

AGE _____ BIRTHDAY _____/_____/_____

BARF1

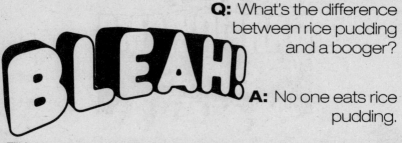

Q: What's the difference between rice pudding and a booger?

A: No one eats rice pudding.

Fill in the consent form below and mail it, along with your joke(s), to:

BDD-BFYR/BARF JOKES
1540 Broadway
New York, NY 10036

TO BDD-BFYR/BARF JOKES:
I am sending you my grossest joke(s) for you to possibly print in
BARF-O-RAMA: THE GROSSEST GROSS JOKE BOOK.

Signed: _____

Name (please print): _____

Street address: _____

City, State, Zip: _____

Birth date: _____/_____/_____

Parent's signature: _____

All jokes submitted become the property of Bantam Doubleday Dell's Books for Young Readers
Division and can be used in any additional books, advertising, or promotion without compensation.

**Your joke will be considered for publication only if your parent or guardian has signed this
consent form. BDD-BFYR may use your joke with or without your name as described above.**

Know any gross jokes?

Tell us your favorite joke—the grosser the better. If your joke
grosses us out, it may appear in

BARF-O-RAMA: THE GROSSEST GROSS JOKE BOOK,
coming in April 1997.